THE DANGER JOE SHOW
Bungee Baboon Rescue

by Jon Buller and Susan Schade

SCHOLASTIC INC.
New York   Toronto   London   Auckland   Sydney
Mexico City   New Delhi   Hong Kong   Buenos Aires

The authors would like to thank Dan Wharton, Director of the Central Park Zoo, for occasionally lending them his brain.

Visit Jon Buller and Susan Schade at their website: www.bullersooz.com

ISBN 0-439-40976-4

12 11 10 9 8 7 6 5 4 3 2 1   2 3 4 5 6 7/0

Printed in the U.S.A.   40

First Scholastic printing, September 2002

For ELLANORA RA[...]
Welcome to the [...]

CHAPTER ONE
JOE, JR., IN AFRICA

Guess what — I'm in *AFRICA!*

I'm sitting on the balcony of our hotel room.

There are two chairs. And a little table. And a vine in a pot.

Dad is out, and I have to stay here until he gets back.

I don't mind.

I'm typing an e-mail to my mom, and I'm using my dad's laptop. He said it was OK.

Dear Mom, I type. **JAMBO. HABARI?**

I chuckle to myself. She'll be surprised to read that. It's in Swahili!

Swahili is a language that is spoken in some parts of Africa.

1

Jambo means "hello." *Habari* means "how are you?"

I know a little Swahili because I have already been in Africa for two weeks.

I'm here with my dad. He's filming an episode of *The Danger Joe Show*. That's a TV show about wild animals. My dad is Danger Joe, and he is the star of the show.

We came to Africa to film baboons in the bush. (In Africa, that's what they call wild places — the bush.) Baboons are so cool. They are a kind of monkey.

I've had a great time, and I can't wait to tell my mom all about it!

I look at what I've written so far.

On the screen it says **JAMBO. HABARI?**

I hunch over the keyboard and type: **That means "Hello. How are you?" in Swahili.**

Now Mom will know what it means.

Then I type: **We got your e-mail about Janie catching a tarantula.**

I stop typing.

I think about Jane, my little sister. I'm really not surprised that Janie caught a tarantula. She is crazy about animals, just like my dad. The two of them will do anything to be close to animals. They never worry about their own safety. So my mom worries about them.

Now she is worrying about Jane's tarantula.

I know about tarantulas. They are big hairy spiders, but they aren't as bad as they look.

I type: The kind of tarantulas that live near our home aren't poisonous to people. But they do have special hairs on them that can make your skin itch, so you shouldn't pick them up with your bare hands.

If Dad was home, he'd say that wild things belong in the wild. He'd tell Jane to think like a tarantula. If she thinks like a big hairy spider, she'll realize that it wouldn't be fun to live in a taco box.

If you tell her that, I think she will let the tarantula go.

I sit back in my chair. I guess that's enough about tarantulas.

I think for a few minutes. Then I type: We finished filming the baboons. They were great. Dad says we might go to Victoria Falls next. He liked bungee jumping so much that . . .

I stop.

I don't know how much Mom knows about bungee jumping. She might think it's dangerous. And then she would worry. You never know with moms.

I highlight the last part, about bungee jumping, and punch the delete button.

I don't think I'll tell Mom about the whole bungee jumping thing. Dad can tell her when we're back home, safe and sound.

I'll tell her about the hippo in my tent, instead. That will make her laugh!

No, wait. Let me think about that. Maybe she wouldn't think it was so funny.

Let's see. I know I shouldn't say anything about the cobra, either. Mom doesn't really like snakes.

Hmmm. There must be *something* I can tell her that won't make her worry.

I think back to the day we arrived in Africa.

That was the day Elton bought the mystery package. . . .

CHAPTER TWO
THE MYSTERY PACKAGE

My first sight of Africa is from an airplane.

We are coming in for a landing, and Dad wakes me up.

I see some tall modern buildings, and some trees, and some roads. It looks like any big city.

After landing, we stand in the airport, looking around. It's Dad and me, and Lucy the producer, and Elton our camera guy.

The airport is mostly full of busy-looking people in normal-looking clothes. I am a little disappointed. I thought Africa was going to be different!

Dad says, "Elton, will you see about our other bags? I'll get a taxi."

He puts his hand on my shoulder. "Joe, Jr.," he says, "come with us. And stay close."

I stay close to Dad and Lucy.

We get a taxi, and we drive away from the airport. I lean forward so I can look out the window.

We're driving along when *hey!* I see something that makes my head whip around.

We just passed three camels walking right down the street! You wouldn't see that in New York! Or in Chicago, either!

"Camels!" Dad says. "Now, there's an animal that's fit for the desert! It has webbed feet for walking on sand, long eyelashes to protect its eyes, and a hump to store fat! One hump, Joe," he says to me. "Do you know what the one-humped camels are called?"

"Yup," I say. "Dromedaries."

"Right! And the two-humped?"

"Um, I forget," I say.

"*Bactrian* camels. I think there are still some

wild Bactrian camels in Asia. I'd love to do a show on them! What do you think, Lucy?"

Lucy is the producer. It's her job to tell Dad what animals he should cover on the show. Of course, she listens to Dad if he has a good idea.

Lucy says she'll look into the Bactrian camels of Asia. Then the taxi stops in front of our hotel.

The hotel has a swimming pool, and our room has a phone. You can call the front desk and ask them to send up potato chips and an ice-cream sandwich, or whatever you want. (Everybody at the hotel speaks English.)

We also have a balcony.

Dad and I hold onto the balcony railing and take big whiffs of the African air. It smells nice.

"That's the smell of eucalyptus," Dad says. "Eucalyptus trees actually come from Australia. You know about koalas, don't you?" he continues. "Those cute little gray animals with fluffy white ears?"

I say, "Yeah, Dad, I know. Janie has a koala stuffed animal. She carries it around all the time."

"That's right, she does," Dad says with a smile. "The reason I brought up koalas is because they live in Australia and eat eucalyptus leaves for all their meals. It's their favorite food."

I take another deep breath. Eucalyptus smells good, but it doesn't smell like food to me.

Lucy knocks on our door. She has a notebook

full of lists — of people to see and things to do. You need to get lots of permission slips to make a film here. Dad calls it "making arrangements."

Dad and Lucy go out to make arrangements. Elton has to stay with me.

He puts his feet on the table and his hands behind his head and looks up at the ceiling.

"Well, what do you want to do?" he asks.

"Let's go out!" I say. I want to see everything. "We should go out and see stuff! Buy stuff!"

Elton sits up straight. "Now you're talking," he says. Elton is from New York. He loves to shop.

He pauses for a second. "You don't think we'll get lost, do you?"

"I don't know," I say. "Why don't you call the front desk and ask them if they have a map or something?"

Elton says, "You call. Ask them, 'Where's the best shopping?'"

"OK." I like calling the front desk. I pick up

the phone and somebody says, "Good morning. How may I help you?"

I say, "Can you tell me where to go to shop for souvenirs and stuff?"

The man on the phone says they "will arrange everything, Mister Denim." (Mister Denim — that means me!) This is a great place!

We go down to the lobby. The front desk shows us where to change our dollars to *birr,* which is the money they use in this part of Africa.

There's a car waiting to take us to the market. Cool!

Our driver has a straw hat and a gray beard. He's wearing shorts and a checkered shirt. His name is Leo.

Leo says, "I will be your driver today."

He holds the door open for us. "I speak English very well, as you can hear. Also," he continues, "I speak Italian and German, and the

African languages of Amharic, Oromifaa, Tigrinya, and Swahili."

Wow!

"Can I sit in the front?" I ask him. "Can you teach me some words?"

I get in. Leo pulls out into traffic.

"You will find that most people you meet in the market speak English," he says. "But the official language here is Amharic. To ask how much, you say, '*Sintinu?*'"

"Sintinu?" I say.

"Good, good! And if you don't like the price, you can say, *'Aydellem.'* That means no."

"And if you decide to buy, you can say, *'Ow,'* for yes."

That makes me laugh. *"Ow* is yes," I say.

"Ow," says Leo, nodding his head.

Leo takes us to the market. He will wait for us. And when we're done, he'll take us back to the hotel.

Elton and I get out of the car.

The market is huge. It smells like coffee beans and sweet spices. People are everywhere. There are more things for sale than you have ever seen in your life!

We look this way and that. People brush past us. People call out to us and try to get us to look at their stuff. There's so much to see!

We move along in the crowd. We walk by lots of booths and tables. I don't have any idea what direction we came from, or where we are, or where we're going!

Soon Elton has bought a couple of bracelets, and a necklace of blue stones, and two pieces of printed cloth, and a silver plate, and some little black pots, and some leather sandals, and a five-foot-high, red-orange-and-yellow basket.

I finally decide to buy a small wooden horse to take home for Jane. "How much?" I ask. I have already forgotten my new words — except *ow*, for yes.

"One hundred birr," the man says, giving me a sly look.

"One hundred birr?!" I say. I frown. I shake my head. "I'll give you twenty."

This is called bargaining. Elton taught me how to do it. The seller says a high price. Then you say a low price. Then he lowers his price a little bit, and you raise yours a little bit. Then you decide on a price in the middle, and everybody is happy.

I buy the horse for Jane. Even though I bargain, it takes most of the money I brought with me.

When I'm done I look for Elton. I don't see him. I start to feel worried. But then something shiny catches my eye. I walk toward it.

It's a statue of a baboon — the animal we came to film!

I walk right up to it. It's gold. Well, probably not *real* gold. I touch it with my finger.

"Ahhh, I see you like the sacred baboon," a woman says to me.

"Sacred?" I ask.

"In ancient Egypt, they worshiped the baboon. They called him Thoth. He was the god of wisdom and of the moon," the woman says. "Do you see his crown? It represents the full moon."

I nod. I can't take my eyes off the statue. A baboon with the full moon on his head! How cool is that? It would look great on my shelf at home. And I could take it to show-and-tell!

I check my pocket. I don't have enough money for a doughnut hole, never mind a baboon statue.

I look around for Elton. Where is he? "Elton!" I call. I look in every direction. *"Where are you?!"*

I finally see him. He is across the market, talking to a man in a *shamma*. That's what a lot

of the people here wear. It's a white cloth that you wrap around yourself.

The man in the shamma is talking a lot. He waves his arms around. He points to the sky, then brings his hand down fast. Then he grins and swings his hand back and forth. Elton is nodding.

What's he buying now? I wonder. (I hope he'll remember to bargain.)

Elton comes up to me. "Wait here," he says. "I'll just be a minute. And keep an eye on these." He plops his packages down next to me and disappears with the guy in the shamma.

Rats. I was going to ask if I could borrow some money to buy the baboon.

I hope he won't be too long. I don't think he's supposed to leave me here all alone.

I'm beginning to get nervous when I spot Leo coming toward me. And then I see Elton, too. They both show up at the same time. They say it's late and we've got to get going. We leave in a hurry.

I don't get to buy my baboon.

Elton shoves a large package into the back of our car. It's wrapped in a green canvas sack and tied up with string.

Then Elton gives the man in the shamma a lot of money. Wow. I didn't even know Elton *had* that much money!

He notices that I'm watching him and turns his back so I can't see.

I'm curious about that mystery package, but Elton doesn't look like he's telling. I try to worm it out of him.

"I saw you talking to that guy in the shamma," I say from the front seat.

"Hmmm," is all Elton has to say.

"What part of Africa is he from?" I try.

Elton laughs. Elton snorts when he laughs. "He's from Seattle!" he says.

Seattle? That makes me feel stupid, so I don't ask him anything else.

When we get to the hotel, Elton takes his packages inside. I wave good-bye to Leo.

"Hey, Joe, Jr.!" Dad calls to me. "Want to come see our safari truck?"

(*Safari* comes from an Arab word. It means journey.)

"*Ow,*" I say.

"What's the matter?" Dad asks.

"Nothing," I say, trying not to laugh.

"Did you hurt yourself?" Dad wants to know.

"No." I have to hold my hand over my mouth.

"Are you OK?"

"*Ow,*" I say again. Then I explain. "*Ow* means yes. But I forget in what language."

Dad laughs. "Good one, Joe," he says. "Was the language Amharic?"

"*Ow!*" I say.

We go to look at the truck.

Whoa! As soon as I see the safari truck, I forget all about Elton's mystery package and the baboon statue that I didn't get.

This is the *coolest* truck I ever saw!

CHAPTER THREE
SAFARI

The safari truck is a custom-made, one-of-a-kind vehicle. It has everything you could want! It's even painted in camouflage!

"Look at this, Joe," Dad says, climbing up to the roof. "This flap folds back to make a rooftop seat!"

I try it out. "This is where *I'm* sitting for the whole trip," I say.

"We'll see," says Dad. "Come on. Check out the inside!"

We climb in, and Dad opens up a door under one of the seats. "Look at all the storage space under here," he says. "And if you prop it open" — he pulls some legs out from under the door flap — "it turns into a sleeping bunk!"

Whoa.

"Looky here! This holds the tents."

Everything flips open, or slides out, or tucks in.

Dad loves it, and so do I!

"Look at this!" He stands on one of the seats and pulls down an overhead door. "A refrigerator!" He pulls down another. "And this is for the medical kit."

He points to the ceiling. "Lights!" he says. He flicks them on and off.

"And that's not all!"

On the outside of the truck, there's a faucet for a shower. And a place for tools. And a cooking grill. And a big fuel tank.

You could live *forever* in this truck!

The next morning, we load her up. Then we all get in, and Dad drives off. *Honk, honk!*

I can't wait to ride on the roof, but Dad says, "Not until we get off the main roads."

It gets hotter and hotter the farther we get from the city. And drier and drier.

After we are off the main roads, we run into a lot of potholes. The truck bounces around so much that I *still* can't ride on the roof.

We pass people walking beside the road with trains of camels. We see people riding on donkeys.

"Ah, domesticated animals," Dad says.

"What?" I say.

"I was just thinking about camels and donkeys," Dad says. "They're *domesticated* animals."

"What does that mean?" I ask.

"It means that they aren't wild. They're tame, and they've been trained to live with humans. People have kept camels for thousands of years. Donkeys not quite as long. But both of them were originally wild animals, like giraffes and zebras."

We pass some children herding goats.

"Look at those goats, Joe," Dad says. "Would you have guessed that they're in the same family as antelopes?"

Dad slows down to take a look.

He says, "Now they are farm animals. They give milk, and in return they get a safe home, and food, and water. "

We stop and watch the goats for a while.

Then we drive on.

We are very far from the city now.

We see a banded mongoose. Dad says it's probably hunting for insects.

We see small round huts in the hills. Dad says they're made out of mud.

I know about mud houses. A lot of houses in

New Mexico are made out of mud. You make bricks out of it and dry them in the sun. Dad says it's the same here.

The sky is big, and there are no clouds. Just dust.

Everything is so bright it makes my eyes sleepy.

We're coming into baboon country now. They call this semidesert. It doesn't rain much. The dirt is kind of reddish brown, with clumps of pale grass. There are a few trees. And some rocky cliffs. It looks like an old Western movie.

Some of the riverbeds are dry. They are called *wadis*. But we will be camping near a big river that has water in it year-round.

The grass is greener here, close to the river, and there are more trees. It's part of a wildlife park.

The safari truck bounces up to some round mud houses, and two men come out to meet us. They are researchers. They study baboons. Every day they follow the baboons and watch what they do. Then they write it all down in a waterproof notebook.

I could do that.

I climb out of the truck.

"This is my son, Joe, Jr.," Dad says. "Joe, this is Dr. Kalal and Tony Maroni."

I say, "Hello. It's nice to meet you."

Tony says, "Hi, Joe, glad you could come."

Dr. Kalal looks at his watch. "Tony," he says, "why don't you show Joe, Jr., around? Be back by three o'clock, and we'll have time to visit the sleeping cliffs."

"Sure thing," says Tony.

I like Tony already.

"C'mon, Joe! Let's go down to the river," Tony says. "Has anyone told you what to watch out for here in the bush?"

"Well, poisonous snakes, I would guess," I say. "They have cobras around here, don't they?"

"That's right. Always look where you're walking, and avoid the tall grass. Snakes like to hang out there."

I follow Tony to the river. The edges are shallow. But in the middle the water is deep. It swirls and bubbles, and the current is fast.

"That's because of the falls," says Tony. "Right around that bend there's a waterfall. You want to be real careful around the river. You don't want to get swept over the falls. But that's not all. You also need to watch out for hippos and crocodiles. Look over there."

We walk a little way, and Tony points to some smooth rocks in the shallow water. "You might think those are rocks, but they're not," he says. "They're hippopotamuses!"

"No way!" I say. "They look just like rocks!"

Tony laughs. "Just keep watching," he says. And after a moment, he points. "There!" The water near one of the rocks swirls around a little and then up pop two ears, two eyes, and two nostrils! "She's coming up for air," says Tony. "They usually come up for air every few minutes, but they *can* stay underwater for up to thirty minutes. They can walk along the river bottom, too."

"Wow. I wish I could do that," I say.

"The best part is that they can close their nostrils, so they don't get water up their nose. Hippos are the coolest animals!"

"You sound like my dad," I say.

Tony laughs again. "Well, that's good, because I think your dad is just about the coolest *human* I know! I hope I can have a show like his someday!"

I'm glad Tony likes my dad.

"The hippos stay in the water pretty much all day," Tony says. "But at night, when it gets cool, they come up on land and eat grass. They look like the sweetest animals, but they aren't. You want to stay away from hippos, and don't get between them and the water when they're on land. It makes them nervous."

Another hippo head comes out of the water. This one turns and looks at us.

"See how brown and murky the water is?" Tony says. "It's too muddy to see what's underneath. You never know — there might be crocodiles!"

"Whoa," I say.

"So, now you know how to stay safe in the bush," says Tony. "Watch out for tall grass and the river, right?"

"Right," I say.

I watch the murky water, hoping I'll see a crocodile, but Tony says it's time to head back.

I follow him up the trail, looking at the clumps of tall grass. No snakes in sight . . . yet.

CHAPTER FOUR
THE SLEEPING CLIFFS

It's time to see the baboons, and Dad is all excited.

We won't film anything today. We'll just check out the place where the baboons go to sleep.

We'll start filming tomorrow.

We walk above the riverbank. I tell Lucy what I learned from Tony. We both keep our eyes peeled for snakes and crocodiles.

Elton keeps stopping to look across the river with his binoculars, and he falls behind.

Dr. Kalal points up the river to some faraway cliffs on the other side. "Those are the sleeping cliffs," he says, "where our baboons come every night.

"Not all baboons sleep on cliffs," he explains to me. "This kind is special. They're known as hamadryas baboons, or desert baboons, since they live in the desert. They are also sometimes called sacred baboons, because they were important in the ancient Egyptian religion."

"Oh, yeah," I say. I remember the statue. "I heard about that — Thoth, the god of wisdom."

I bet Dr. Kalal is surprised I know that!

We walk on.

"Look, Joe!" Dad says.

I look where he's pointing, and I see a small brown animal disappearing into some rocks.

"A rock hyrax!" Dad says. "There's another! They look a little like the hoary marmots that we saw at Mosquito Lake."

This time I use *my* binoculars. It does look sort of like a hoary marmot, or a really big guinea pig. "I see it!" I say.

"Would you believe the rock hyrax is more closely related to an elephant than to a marmot?" Dad says.

An elephant? But elephants are huge and have gray skin. And these animals are little and furry! If it was anybody but Dad who said they were related, I wouldn't believe it. But my dad knows his animals.

We're climbing now, getting higher and higher above the river. The cliffs rise up on both sides. The water below is running fast, and it's a long drop.

I hope we don't have to go too near the edge.

Dr. Kalal says in a quiet voice, "We can stop here." He squats down, and we do the same. And we all look at the opposite cliff through our binoculars.

"See those dark marks on the face of the cliff?" Dr. Kalal says. "Those are baboon droppings. That's where the baboons sleep."

"What?!" I say. "You mean right on the side of the cliff?!"

I can't believe it!

Tony and Dad both smile at me. Tony says, "You'll see. They sleep there to stay safe from leopards."

"LEOPARDS!" Dad exclaims. "Now, *there's* a beautiful animal! What are our chances of spotting a leopard?" he asks.

"Not too good," says Tony. "I've been watching the baboons for over a year now, and I've never seen a leopard. There aren't many left in these parts, and they're very secretive animals to start with." Then Tony gets embarrassed. "Oh, but I guess you know that, sir," he says.

Lucy says, "Do the baboons have any other enemies?"

"Sure," says Tony. "Besides leopards, there are hyenas, wild dogs, and crocodiles."

Lucy writes this down in her notebook.

"Sometimes an eagle will snatch up a baby baboon," Dr. Kalal adds.

Dad says, "Listen! What's that?"

I listen, but I don't hear anything.

I look around with my binoculars.

Then *YEEEK!* I hear a piercing little shriek!

"Baby baboon!" whispers Dad.

And then there's a deep, rumbly sound.

"Soothing papa baboon," Dad says. "He's telling the baby not to worry, Papa is close by."

He touches my arm and points.

I look with the binoculars. It's my first sight of a real, live baboon.

"It's a male," Dad says. "See that thick silvery fur on his shoulders? That's particular to the male desert baboon. The female doesn't have it. Her fur is much shorter and plain brown."

The male sits on top of the cliff with his hands between his knees and stares at us. He looks like the statue in the market.

He makes a loud call. *BAAAAHUU!*

Then he starts climbing. Right down the face of the cliff! He holds on with his fingers and toes, and he uses his tail to brace himself.

I hold my breath. But he doesn't fall.

More baboons follow. Some of the females have babies clinging to them. They all scurry down the cliff. Little groups scrunch close together on the ledges. Even when there's hardly any room.

"Those are families," Dad explains. "See

how there's one male and several females in each group?"

Some of the younger males sit by themselves. Dad points one out to me.

"He's got more room," Dad says, "but he won't be as warm in the night."

More and more baboons come. Some come from one side of the cliff and some from the other. More baboons climb up the cliff from down by the river.

We watch until it's almost dark, and the baboons are all huddled close to the face of the cliff. I can't believe they sleep like that, but they do.

Then, like the baboons, we walk back to *our* sleeping place — the camp. And we go to sleep, too.

CHAPTER FIVE
BABOON BEHAVIOR

It's day two at the camp. Before light.

Today, we're going to film baboons. We'll be starting where we left off last night — at the sleeping cliffs.

When we get there, I can just make out the dark shapes of the baboons on the other side of the river. They're starting to leave their sleeping spots and climb up the face of the cliff.

"They hang out on top of the sleeping cliffs for a while," Tony tells me. "Then they go off to hunt for food."

Elton starts filming.

"THAT'S A WHOLE HECK OF A LOT OF BABOONS!" Dad says in his loud television

43

whisper. Dad isn't in the picture, but Elton is recording his voice over the sounds of the baboons. The rest of us aren't supposed to make any noise at all.

"THERE MUST BE A HUNDRED OF THEM!" Dad whispers. "OR MORE! THEY SLEEP ON THE FACE OF THESE CLIFFS, WHERE THEIR ENEMIES CAN'T GET THEM. AND THEN THEY RISE WITH THE SUN!"

He's right. By the time the sun is shining on the cliff, all of the baboons are up. The young ones are playing, and the older ones are grooming each other. I look through my binoculars.

"WATCH THE GROOMING BEHAVIOR," Danger Joe continues. "GROOMING IS AN IMPORTANT SIGN OF LOVE AND RESPECT AMONG BABOONS. YOU'LL FIND THAT MOST OF THE GROOMING GOES ON WITHIN THE FAMILY."

Grooming is something baboons do a lot. It's when they comb through each other's hair with their fingers, looking for bugs and sticks and stuff. It's like when Mom straightens Dad's tie.

I like the baby baboons. The littlest ones have black fur and pale faces. The older ones are brown like their mothers. They all look like little hairy wrinkled old men.

I see a baby climb over the back of a big male. The male hugs it, and the mother watches, making nervous noises.

"LOOK AT THAT!" says Danger Joe. "THEY REALLY LOVE THEIR BABIES, DON'T THEY?"

Elton slowly sweeps the big camera from left to right, across the whole scene.

Tony touches Dad's arm and points to some baboons that are moving away from the group. Dad nods. Lucy shows Elton where to direct the camera. They don't talk because the tape is recording.

Danger Joe is the only one talking. "THIS WHOLE GROUP OF BABOONS IS CALLED A

TROOP," he says. "NOW THEY WILL GO LOOKING FOR FOOD. THE TROOP WILL DIVIDE INTO SMALLER GROUPS BECAUSE THERE ISN'T ENOUGH FOOD FOR ALL OF THEM TO EAT IN ONE PLACE."

The baboons are moving off in different directions. Dad continues, "LET'S THINK LIKE BABOONS NOW, AND SEE IF WE CAN CATCH UP WITH ONE OF THE FAMILIES!"

Dad is always telling people to think like

animals. Well, I bet I know what those baboons are thinking now. *Let's find something to eat!*

The baboons disappear over the ridge, and we rush down our side of the cliff.

Dr. Kalal leads the way.

We come to a rope-and-log bridge.

Dr. Kalal crosses the bridge. Tony and Dad and Lucy follow him.

I step on the first log. I can feel the whole bridge swaying back and forth.

Elton is behind me, carrying his camera equipment. "Oh, no!" he says. "No way! You've gotta be kidding!"

I cross the bridge.

Elton says, "Where's the real bridge? I'll go around."

Of course, there is no real bridge. This is it!

In the end, Elton makes it across. But he's sweating a lot when he gets to the other side.

The sun moves up in the sky, and it gets hotter and hotter.

Finally, we find a family of baboons.

The head baboon watches us.

Dr. Kalal knows how close the head baboon will let us get to his family. Of course, Dad tries to get closer, but Dr. Kalal says, "That's close enough!" So Dad has to stay back.

They start filming the baboon family.

Dad says, "EACH BABOON FAMILY IS MADE UP OF A DOMINANT, OR HEAD,

MALE, ABOUT TEN FEMALES, AND THEIR CHILDREN. AND THERE MAY ALSO BE ONE OR TWO YOUNG MALES, CALLED FOLLOWERS."

The head baboon yawns.

"GOOD GOLLY!" says Dad. "LOOK AT THOSE TEETH!"

The baboons have behinds that are completely bare, with no hair on them at all. And their butts are bright pink! It makes them look like they have on one-piece pajamas — the kind with a flap in the back. And the flap is open.

It's kind of embarrassing.

We follow the baboons for most of the day. They cover a lot of ground. Every time they come to a good spot, they stop and have something to eat — leaves, or roots, or insects.

I think like a baboon. When they stop to eat, I stop and take a snack out of my pack. Gummy worms.

Elton films. Dad talks about baboons. Tony and Dr. Kalal take notes.

It gets to be over one hundred degrees. Sometimes the baboons stop under a big acacia tree and get some shade. But we have to keep our distance, so we're still stuck out in the sun. There just aren't that many trees around here.

The baboons know we're nearby. I wonder what they think of us, standing out in the sun while they rest in the shade and eat acacia leaves.

"SEE THAT FELLOW SITTING OFF BY HIMSELF?" Dad says to the camera. "THAT'S A FOLLOWER. IT WILL BE SEVERAL YEARS BEFORE HE HAS A FAMILY OF HIS OWN."

I look at the follower, and I feel sorry for him. All the females are grooming the big, older male. I think the follower must feel lonely.

By the time we're ready to head back to the camp, I'm all limp. I can hardly walk. I'm tired of thinking like a baboon.

"You're weak from the heat," says Dad. He doesn't look weak. He doesn't even look hot.

He squats down and taps his shoulder. "Climb up," he says. "All juvenile baboons get rides."

So now I'm a juvenile baboon.

Actually, I love to ride on Dad's shoulders.

I say, "I like the way some of the babies ride on their mother's back, leaning against her tail."

"Sorry. I don't have a tail," says Dad.

From high up on Dad's shoulders, I look back and see Elton. It seems to me like he is falling farther and farther behind.

"Dad," I say. "Is Elton like a follower?"

"A follower? Like in the baboon family? Well, in some ways, I suppose. He is a young male. And he doesn't have his own family yet. But he's part of the *Danger Joe Show* family."

Dad stops walking, and we wait for Elton to catch up.

Later, after supper, Dad says, "Hey, Joe, why

don't you go and see how Elton is feeling? He's not used to the heat."

"OK."

I trot over to Elton's tent. The flap is open, so I pop in.

Elton is squatting over a pile of rope or something. He gasps, pulls a blanket over it, and yells at me. "What are you doing in here?! Can't a guy get any privacy?!"

"Sorry," I say with a gulp and back out.

"No, wait!" Elton grabs me by the wrist.

He glares at me.

"How much did you see?!" he asks.

CHAPTER SIX
JUMPING HIPPOS

Elton pulls me into his tent and sits me down on his cot.

He stands with his arms folded over his chest, eyeing me.

I squirm around and look sideways.

I see the green canvas sack that was wrapped around Elton's mystery package. It's empty now.

"Can you keep a secret?" Elton asks.

Then he grins. He can't hold it in. He's probably been dying to tell somebody for days!

Whew! For a minute there he was kind of scary. Now he's just Elton.

"Of course!" I say. "You can tell me."

"This is serious," Elton says. "You've got to promise not to tell anybody."

"OK," I say.

"Say it," Elton says. He's not taking any chances.

"I promise not to tell anybody," I say.

"Not even your dad," says Elton.

"Not even my dad," I say.

"Spit on it," says Elton.

"Spit on it?" I ask.

"Yeah, to seal the promise. Spit in your hand."

Gross! I never heard of that before. But I spit into my hand, knowing this must be a good secret. I put out my hand to shake with Elton.

"What are you doing?" he asks.

"Don't we have to shake now?"

"Eww. No, dude. You just spit," he says.

Oh. I rub my hand on my jeans. They're all covered with dirt anyway.

"OK," says Elton. "Look."

He lifts up the blanket.

I look, but I don't get it. "Uh, what is it?" I ask.

"It's a bungee cord!"

I must look like I don't understand, because Elton explains it to me.

"You know," he says, "for bungee jumping! Where you jump off a high place, and the cord keeps you from hitting the ground. It's the coolest sport! I know some guys who do it all the time! Look!"

His eyes are shining. He lifts up one end of the cord and pulls it to show me how stretchy it is. "And I got a great deal on it, too!" he says.

I look at him with my mouth hanging open. This is a guy who doesn't like to cross the river on a rope-and-log bridge. And he's going to *bungee jump*?! With a bungee cord that he got *on sale*?

"Surprised you, huh?" says Elton. "There's a jumping shelf a little way past the sleeping cliffs," he says. "It's made out of steel! Nothing could be safer!"

Who does he think I am? His mother?

Elton says. "Sam used to operate a jump site there. He told me all about it. He even gave me a map!"

Elton unfolds a map and shows it to me.

"Is Sam the guy in the shamma? The one who sold you this stuff?"

"Yeah. Sam, from Seattle."

I look at the map.

I see the rope bridge, and the sleeping cliffs, and a dotted line that goes to a drawing of a tree with a crooked trunk. Then there's a dotted line that goes to a bush or something. And near the bush there's a big X.

"Cool!" I say. I think of something. "When are you going to jump? Won't you be busy filming all the time?"

"Probably not the whole time," Elton says. "Things come up."

That reminds me. "Dad sent me to see how you are feeling," I say.

"Oh, I feel fine now," Elton says. "Thanks for asking."

I get off the cot.

"And don't forget, Joe, Jr.," Elton says. "You made a promise! And you spit on it!"

I wonder what happens if you break a promise that you spit on.

I go back to my dad.

I say, "Elton said he feels fine."

I'm dying to tell Dad about Elton's bungee stuff, but I promised I wouldn't. And I spit on it.

So I go to bed.

I have a dream:

I'm lying on top of the murky river, but I don't sink and I don't feel wet. It's sort of like being in bed. I don't even worry about crocodiles. In fact, I think I might be a crocodile!

Above me are the sleeping cliffs. I see a bunch of

hippos looking over the edge. They open their big mouths. They are laughing.

Then one of them jumps! Right toward me!

But I'm not worried, because I can see that the hippo's attached to a bungee cord.

The hippos are bungee jumping!

That makes me laugh, and I wake myself up.

I untwist my tangled blanket.

Then I hear a noise outside the tent. A kind of *thump!*

My heart starts pounding.

I look over and see my dad sleeping beside me. He doesn't hear it.

Something brushes against the side of the tent.

I gasp and hold my breath.

I see the tent fabric move. Something's at the front flap!

The flap starts to open. . . .

Something's coming into our tent!

CHAPTER SEVEN
THE SPITTING COBRA

"YAAAAAAAAAAAH!" I scream at the top of my lungs.

I leap out of bed!

My father leaps out of bed!

The tent falls down on our heads!

We can't see anything. The tent is all over us. There's a lot of noise. My father grabs me. He slices open the back of the tent with his knife and we crawl out.

The others are crowding around in their pajamas. Then somebody starts laughing.

And Dad starts laughing.

And then I see a huge gray backside waddling away from us and down toward the river.

"WHERE'S A CAMERA?!" Dad shouts. "HAS ANYBODY GOT A CAMERA?!"

It's a hippo, and he's wearing a huge piece of our tent on his head!

Dad and I sleep the rest of the night in the safari truck.

The next morning I wake up. For a minute I feel confused.

What time is it? Why am I in the safari truck?

Where am I? Oh, yeah, I'm in the safari truck.

Why didn't anybody wake me up?

Then I remember the hippo in our tent. I was scared then, but it's funny now.

I get up and start putting on my clothes.

I pull on one sock.

I start thinking about the day before, and I remember Elton's secret.

I pull on the other sock.

I don't really like keeping a secret from my dad. He wouldn't like it, either, if he knew about it.

But what do they expect from a kid, anyway?! You aren't supposed to have secrets from your dad. But you aren't supposed to break a promise, either. Or be a tattletale. Right?

Besides, if I told on Elton, Dad probably wouldn't let him go bungee jumping. And I *want* him to go. It sounds so cool.

I don't think I want to bungee jump myself. Kids aren't allowed to, anyway. It's one of those "don't try this in your own backyard" things. Like picking up snakes or petting wild animals.

But still, it would be fun to watch!

I raid the food cupboard in the truck, and then I go outside.

I find Dad looking at our torn tent and at the trampled grass and bushes around it.

"Mornin', son," he says. "Last night was kind of rough, huh? I've been thinking. Let's take today off. We don't have to film *every* day. We can hang around here and relax. Elton says he wouldn't mind catching up on his sleep. And Dr. Kalal has already left to follow the baboons.

I thought we could go down to the river and take a look at those hippos!"

Aha! I should have known Dad would be interested in the hippos after last night.

"Great!" I say. "Let's go see the hippos!"

Tony and Lucy want to come, too.

Lucy brings her notebook and video camera. You never know what you might want to film.

We find the hippos easily. They're in the

river, trying to stay cool because it's already getting hot. There are about six of them, just lolling around, half in and half out of the water.

There's even a baby hippo.

"Look at that little guy!" says Dad. "He must weigh three hundred pounds!"

The baby hippo moves around a lot more than the adults. He makes little grunts and bellows, and swims back and forth. He climbs on

the big hippos' backs and rolls off, splashing into the water.

"Oh, isn't that cute?" cries Lucy. "It reminds me of Suni." She starts filming.

Suni is Lucy's baby girl. She's almost two. Lucy misses her a lot when we go on a trip.

Dad is squatting down at the edge of the river, watching. He likes to get as close as he can to the animals, even when he's not making a film. He imagines what it's like — to be a hippo in muddy water, for instance. He can think about it for a long time.

All of a sudden, Tony dashes up to Dad and smacks the water near him with a big stick!

There's a huge splash. Dad falls backward on his butt, sopping wet, and a huge crocodile tail lashes out of the water!

Dad says, *"Woo hoo!* Would you look at the size of that croc! What a whopper!"

"I'm so sorry I splashed you, sir," says Tony to Dad. "I just —"

"Hey," says Dad, "call me Joe. And there's no need to apologize, Tony. That was quick thinking. Thanks! I had no idea I was so close to such a fine beast. I just wish I had my mask and snorkel!" he adds.

I think, *It's a good thing he doesn't!* The last thing we need is for Dad to dive into the river.

Tony is looking at my dad with his mouth open. He whistles through his teeth. *Phweeeeuw!* "You wouldn't *really* swim in there would you, sir? I mean, Joe?"

Dad just laughs. "What other animals have you seen around here, Tony?"

"Jackals," says Tony. "Hyenas. Water turtles. Mole rats. Ants. Ticks. Crickets. Lizards. Cobras."

They talk snakes for a long time.

Then, on the way back to the camp, Tony spots one.

"Look! Snake!" he cries. And he runs after it!

Dad follows him. They go leaping through the tall grass, whooping and chasing the snake.

"He's really moving!" says Dad as he runs. "And how about their camouflage! That reddish-brown color blends right in with the dirt and the grass. Did you see where he went?"

They stop. I hear Tony whisper, "He's in there." Tony carefully pushes apart a clump of tall grass, and *zap!* A spray of venom shoots out at his face!

It's a spitting cobra, and it gets Tony in the eyes. That's what spitting cobras do.

This is serious. We all rush back to camp.

Tony is stumbling and holding his eyes. He says, "Sorry, guys. That was so stupid!" There are tears running down his face. His eyes must sting like crazy.

Lucy unpacks the emergency medical kit. Dad washes Tony's eyes with lots of water, and Lucy puts some drops of medicine in them.

Tony's eyes should be OK now, because he got the medicine right away. But Dad decides to drive him to the medical center, just to make sure. Lucy rides with Tony.

"Stay here, Joe," Dad says to me. "We won't be more than a few hours. Dr. Kalal will be back soon. And Elton is here, of course. Go find him."

In all the excitement I had forgotten about Elton.

I hurry to Elton's tent.

He's not there.

And neither is his bungee cord!

CHAPTER EIGHT
ELTON ON THE CLIFF

I don't have to think twice. I head for the cliffs. I'm supposed to find Elton, right?

Besides, I never saw anybody bungee jump before!

I don't even feel guilty anymore about not telling Dad. I couldn't tell him even if I wanted to, because he isn't here!

I don't walk through any clumps of tall grass. And I'm careful not to get too close to the river.

After a while, I stop and scan the cliffs on the other side of the river with my binoculars. There he is! I see Elton! He's climbing up the side of the sleeping cliffs. And he's lugging the green canvas sack.

I cross the rope-and-log bridge. I can see the water rushing beneath my feet. I step carefully from log to log.

Then I climb along the side of the cliff. *Huff, huff.* I can't see Elton anymore.

I call out, "Elton! Wait up!" But he doesn't hear me.

The sun is hot, hot, hot.

But I remembered my water bottle. I stop for a long drink.

I hurry along the top of the sleeping cliffs. There's a lot of baboon poop up here.

I'm panting hard.

I see a tree. It has a crooked trunk. There aren't very many trees up here, so I think it must be the one on the map. From there it's a short walk to the bush.

Now I see the jumping shelf, sticking out over the cliff like a diving board.

But where's Elton? Did he jump already?

Oh. There he is. Lying on the shelf.

What's he doing?

He's lying flat, holding onto the shelf so tightly that his knuckles are white. His eyes are squeezed shut.

Then I figure it out.

He's scared to death. He isn't *doing* anything because he's afraid to move!

I guess Elton has a fear of heights. A lot of people do.

"Elton!" I call. He doesn't even hear me.

I rush up beside the shelf and start talking. I try to sound calm.

"Elton, it's me, Joe, Jr. It's time to come back now. Can you open your eyes? Look at me, Elton."

He doesn't move or open his eyes.

I try to act like the cops on an emergency rescue show on TV. You're supposed to talk in a soothing voice.

I just keep talking. I tell him about the hippos that we saw and about the spitting cobra. After a while I get him to open his eyes and look at me.

"That's good," I say. "Don't look down. Don't take your eyes off me."

Elton looks down.

Sheesh! Why can't people do what you tell them?

"ELTON!" I yell. "I say, 'Don't look down!' and the first thing you do is look down! This isn't easy, you know!"

Hmmm. That wasn't exactly a soothing voice.

"Now, pay attention," I say more calmly. "The platform is safe. It's made out of steel. Remember? You can let go with one hand. Just loosen your fingers a little bit."

He loosens his fingers. Maybe yelling at him did the trick after all.

"That's right. See? You won't fall," I say. "Now slide that hand toward me and hold on again. Good. Now the other hand. Just relax your fingers."

It takes a long time for Elton to inch his way toward me, but finally he's back on solid ground. He lies there for a while, like he doesn't have any strength left in his body. Then he sits up and undoes the leg straps.

"Whew!" he says in a shaky voice. "Thanks, Joe, Jr."

He scoots away from the cliff. "You know what I was thinking?" he says. "I was thinking about those baboons coming back and finding me there."

We both look at the sun in the sky.

It's getting late. The baboons will be coming back soon. We have to get the bungee cord and get back to camp.

Neither one of us notices my dad approaching until we hear him yell "ELTON!" in his deep booming television voice.

We both jump and turn around.

"WHAT'S GOING ON HERE?" Dad asks.

Elton's mouth is opening and shutting, but no sounds are coming out. He looks like a fish.

He sort of waves his arm around. "Uh, . . . well . . . I was just . . . um . . ."

I look up toward the sun. It's pretty low in the west. I think it must be time for those baboons to be coming back toward their sleeping cliffs.

"Uh, Dad?" I start.

But before I can continue, we hear one of those piercing little shrieks that baby baboons make.

The baboons are returning!

I look all around, but I don't see any of them on the top of the cliff yet.

I look at Dad.

There's another shriek, louder and more adult.

Where are they?

More shrieks. I can tell now. The sounds are coming from down below.

All three of us rush to the edge of the cliff. Well, Elton sort of hangs back a little. I guess he doesn't like the idea of getting too close to the edge.

We look down.

Something must be wrong. The baboons didn't sound like this last night!

We see a mother baboon rushing back and forth alongside the river. Every few seconds she lets out a loud screech.

The male is nearby, but he isn't looking at her. He's looking at the river.

"Look!" I shout, pointing. "It's one of the baby baboons!"

A tiny baboon is in the river, clinging to a floating log.

The mother is afraid to go after it. But the log is bobbing away from her.

Oh no! It's being swept out into the center of the river. And once it makes it to the center, the fast-moving water will carry it down the river, around the bend, and over the falls!

CHAPTER NINE
DANGER JOE JUMPS!

Dad doesn't hesitate for one second.

He rushes over to the bungee jumping shelf and begins snapping the harnesses around his ankles.

"Dad! What are you doing?" I say. "Wait! Don't jump! What if something goes wrong?! What if the cord breaks?! You're a lot heavier than Elton. Besides, your my *dad*!! Dads don't bungee jump! What if . . . !?"

It's no use.

Dad tests the buckles and the cord and stands on the end of the platform.

"Don't worry about me, son," he says. "Remember, I'm . . ."

That's my dad, soaring through the air! His arms are spread out like an eagle's wings, and he's diving right toward the center of the river, where the baby baboon is hanging onto its log.

The bungee cord flaps around loose behind him. Then it straightens. Then it begins to stretch out.

Down and down he goes.

He hits the water in front of the baby baboon with a splash. And then he disappears into the river!

YOW!

I knew it! I knew something would go wrong!

But wait! He's coming up.

There are his feet, his knees, his arms.

Even before his head is out of the water, he grabs the baby baboon and keeps coming up, pulled back by the bungee cord.

Up, up, up! Almost back to the platform. But

not quite. They hang in midair for a second, then down they go again. But not as far this time — not into the river.

They bounce up again. And down again. And finally they start to swing back and forth, hanging there, upside down, over the water.

The baby baboon is clinging to Dad.

The mother baboon is running back and forth down below, shrieking and looking up at her baby. More baboons are showing up. Lots of them. Some of them hang back and look nervous. Some of them shriek and rush around. A few of them have climbed partway up the cliff to get a better look.

What happens now?

"Elton!" yells Dad. "Hey, Elton! How do we get back up?"

I look at Elton.

Elton looks blank.

"There must be a rope or something!" I say. "How were *you* going to get up?"

Elton just shrugs his shoulders. "I dunno," he says. "I didn't think about that."

I look at the stuff Elton has left lying around on the cliff. There's a long rope with knots in it.

"Is this it?" I ask Elton.

"Oh," says Elton. "I wondered what that was for!"

"Hey!" yells Danger Joe. "What's going on up there?"

"Hang on, Dad," I yell back.

I'm uncoiling the knotted rope, but I don't know what to do with it.

I see that it has big clips on the ends. I guess I can clip one end to the shelf. Except that will mean going out there. Gulp!

There's no point trying to get Elton to do it. Not after all the trouble I had getting him back on solid ground!

I swallow hard. Well, somebody's got to do it. I guess that means me!

I take the end of the rope and start crawling out on my hands and knees.

"WAIT!" says Elton. "Wait, Joe," he says to me. "You're too little. *I'll* go."

I think that's one of the bravest things I've ever heard — from someone with a fear of heights.

Elton comes a few steps toward me, takes a nervous peek at the edge of the cliff, turns green, and starts swaying back and forth.

"That's all right, Elton," I say. "I'm not afraid of heights. I can do it."

"Oh, boy," breathes Elton, backing up again. "I guess it's gotta be you, Joe, Jr. But wait, let me get this safety rope around you. I can't have anything happen to you."

I let him hook me up to the safety rope.

"Hurry up," I say.

Finally, I crawl out on the jumping shelf.

At the end of the shelf, there are some sturdy

rings. I hope this is what they're for. I attach a
clip to one of them.

I'm about to throw the rope down when I
think, *What if it hits Dad on the head?* I hook the
other clip around the bungee cord instead, so it
will slide down the cord. And then I feed the
knotted rope down the bungee cord to Dad.

He sees what I'm doing. "Good going, Joe!"
he calls up. "That's my boy!"

I inch my way back off the platform.

I think of something. "Elton," I say. "If you had jumped all by yourself, you wouldn't have been able to get back up again! You'd be hanging upside down until somebody found you!"

"Gosh, dude, you're right!" says Elton.

Dad climbs over the platform. It's a good thing he's strong.

The baby baboon is holding on tight to Dad's neck and making little whimpering noises. "That's OK, little fella, you're safe now," Dad says, comforting him.

The baby pulls on Dad's hair. Dad makes some low, murmuring noises, like a papa baboon.

"That's great! Hold it just like that!"

It's Lucy, the producer. She came from out of nowhere! She's pointing her camcorder at Dad. "That was an *awesome* sequence!" she says. "And I got the whole thing on film!"

Dad is all smiles. The baby baboon climbs onto his back. He plays with it until it calms

down. Lucy keeps filming. Everything seems like it's going to be fine, then . . .

B A A A A H U U!

YIKES! It's an adult male baboon! With a scared-looking female right behind him. I had forgotten all about the parents!

"OK," Dad says. "It's time to give the baby back. Elton, you and Joe go down the other side of the cliffs. I'll come in a minute."

Dad sounds so serious. It makes me nervous.

We back away, watching as we go. But I don't go too far. What if Dad needs me?

Lucy hangs back with the camera.

Dad sits down, turning his back to the big baboon. "IF I DON'T LOOK AT HIM, HE'LL KNOW I'M NOT A THREAT, AND THAT I DON'T WANT TO HURT HIM," he says to the camera. Then he grins. "AT LEAST I HOPE SO!" he adds.

I hold my breath.

He sets the baby baboon on the ground. "TIME TO GO BACK TO MOMMY AND DADDY, LITTLE BUDDY."

EEEECH! It's the mother calling.

The baby looks up and sees her. He leaps from Dad's back and runs to her.

The big male looks at Dad. He takes the baby from the mother. He holds the baby up in the air for a minute. Then he brings it down and hugs it. The mother starts to groom the baby.

I start breathing again.

Dad gets up slowly and walks toward us, away from the baboons. And he's got a big smile on his face. Lucy gives him a thumbs-up sign.

"That was amazing!" he says. "I never thought I'd get to hold a baby baboon and bungee jump in the same day!"

We start heading down the cliff.

Elton hangs his head. "Uh, Joe? And Joe, Jr. Thanks, guys. You really helped me out."

"Of course, Elton," Danger Joe says. "That's our job, to look out for each other. You know you're like family."

I'm glad Elton is OK. I'm glad Dad is OK. I'm glad Lucy got it all on film. I think we're taking pretty good care of each other.

When we're almost back at the camp, Dad says, "Um, Elton? I don't think it's such a good idea to go bungee jumping on your own. But I hear there's a good professional setup where you can bungee jump off the railroad bridge by Victoria Falls! Now, *that* would be fun! What do you say we have a go?"

Elton looks sort of sick. "Uh, no thanks, Joe," he says. "I don't think bungee jumping is my sport."

Dad looks surprised. "Well, OK. Then I'll race you guys to the safari truck. First one there gets to ride on top."

I'm already way ahead of them.

CHAPTER TEN
MY SOUVENIR

So that's what happened when we were in the bush, filming the baboons.

Back on the hotel balcony, I look down at the screen of Dad's laptop. I haven't gotten very far in my e-mail to Mom. Let's see . . .

I type: **Dad rented a cool truck. It had a seat on the roof! I got to ride up there a few times, but just around the camp.**

I hear a voice I recognize.

"*GADZOOKS!* ISN'T THAT A WHITE SPOTTED GECKO?!"

Dad's back.

"LOOK HOW HE'S ALMOST THE SAME

COLOR AS THE TREE TRUNK. GREAT CAMOUFLAGE!"

I put the laptop on the table and look over the balcony.

Dad and Elton are down there by the pool. The gecko is crawling from Dad's palm onto the branches of a tree.

"So, Elton," Dad's saying, "did you manage to return that bungee cord to Sam?"

"I couldn't find him," Elton says. "But I found someone in the marketplace to trade with me, since I won't be bungee jumping again anytime soon."

"Well, that's good," Dad says.

"Yeah, but all I could get for it was this crazy statue."

Did I hear right? A statue?

Elton dives into his bag and pulls out a small object wrapped in paper. He unwraps it and shows it to Dad. "Do you think Joe, Jr., would want it?" he asks.

I'm leaning way over the balcony railing so I can see better.

It looks like Elton is showing Dad a small gold statue, a gold statue of a baboon with the full moon on his head — the sacred baboon!

"Yes!" I yell from the balcony. "Joe, Jr., does want it!"

Dad and Elton turn to look at me. They both smile and then come into the hotel.

I look at my e-mail and decide to cut it short.

I type: We've all had a great time! I'll see you soon. Love from your son, Joe, Jr.

DANGER JOE'S CREATURE FEATURE:
HAMADRYAS BABOONS

N.O. Tomalin/Bruce Coleman Inc.

BABOONS are large monkeys with long snouts. They move on all fours and spend more time on the ground than in trees. Some people call them "the doglike monkeys."

Baboons eat plant seeds, roots, pods, and flowers, as well as insects and small mammals.

There are several different kinds of baboons. The kind featured in this book is the hamadryas baboon.

Hamadryas baboons are sometimes called desert baboons because of where they live — in dry, rocky, semidesert areas of Ethiopia and Somalia, two countries in Africa, and Saudi Arabia, a country in Southwest Asia.

And sometimes they are called sacred baboons, because they represented Thoth, the god of wisdom, in ancient Egypt.

Hamadryas baboons can be recognized by the bright, pinky-red skin on their faces and rears, and also by the silvery fur on the head and shoulders of full-grown males.

Male hamadryas baboons are twice as big as females. They are strong, swift, and protective of their families. But they will also take food from their females and scold them with threats and quick bites on the neck.

Researchers studying hamadryas baboons

have learned that each head male has a family of one to ten females and their children.

Young adult males who stay with the family are called "followers." When they get older, they will have families of their own.

Several families together make a "clan." The families in one clan sometimes gather food together and sleep near each other.

In the middle of the day, several clans will gather at the water hole. These groups of clans are called "bands." And when more than one band gets together, as they do at the sleeping cliffs, it is called a "troop" of baboons.

It's interesting to study baboons! Some of the things they do are the same things we humans do — like carrying their babies on long walks. And some aren't — like giving the females in their family big bites on the neck when they fall too far behind!

DANGER JOE'S CREATURE FEATURE:
HIPPOPOTAMUSES

Leonard Lee Rue/Photo Researchers, Inc.

Everything about a **HIPPOPOTAMUS** is BIG! Hippos are the second largest land animal on Earth, after elephants. Adult hippos usually weigh from three thousand to eight thousand pounds. Their newborn babies weigh about fifty pounds and are about three feet long.

Hippos also have the second largest mouth

of any animal, after whales. And they have some very big teeth. Their two lower "canine" teeth can be a foot-and-a-half long.

In the wild, hippos live only in Africa. They spend most of their time in rivers and lakes, with just their eyes, ears, and nostrils sticking out above the water. They have to stay wet because the hot sun can dry out their skin and cause it to crack. They do have an oily substance that comes out of their pores to help condition their skin. It is called "blood sweat" because it has a pinkish color to it.

Hippos are plant-eaters. In the daytime they eat underwater plants, and at night they feed mostly on land. They eat between fifteen and sixty pounds of food a day.

Even though they are enormous and shaped like barrels on short legs, hippos can run more than forty miles an hour for long distances. You don't want to get in the way of an oncoming hippo!

DANGER JOE'S WILD WORDS

ACACIA: There are many different kinds of acacia plants. The thorny acacia trees and shrubs that grow in the dry, semidesert areas of eastern Africa are important plant foods for baboons.

AMHARIC: Amharic is the language of the Amhara people. It is the most widely spoken language in Ethiopia.

ANTELOPE: Antelopes are swift-running animals with hooves and horns. They range in size from the tiny royal antelope (three to six pounds) to the giant eland (up to two thousand pounds).

BANDED MONGOOSE: Mongooses are small, fast-moving mammals that live in Africa, Asia, and Madagascar. The banded mongoose has stripes across its back and shoulders. Its diet includes insects, spiders, lizards, snakes, small mammals, birds, eggs, and fruit.

CAMEL: Camels are large, long-necked, tan-colored animals. Desert peoples have used them for thousands of years to carry heavy loads, and for meat, wool, and milk. Camels have humps in which their bodies store fat. That helps them go for long periods without food or water.

CAMOUFLAGE: Camouflage is the use of colors and patterns for hiding. Some animals are naturally camouflaged by having fur or skin that blends in with the background. And some people camouflage their vehicles or their clothing with blotches of brown and green and tan.

COBRA: Cobras are poisonous snakes that live in Africa and Asia. There are different kinds of cobras, and their coloring varies depending on where they live. Some cobras defend themselves by spitting venom (poison) out of the front of their fangs.

CROCODILE: Crocodiles are large, flesh-eating reptiles that live mostly in water. They are closely related to dinosaurs and have long, powerful tails, short legs, huge jaws, and tough, scaly hides. Because crocodiles are fierce hunters, they have few natural enemies.

EUCALYPTUS: Eucalyptus trees come from Australia, but they have been planted around the world. They grow very fast (up to forty-five feet in two years!) and are an important source of wood and oils. Eucalyptus leaves are also the main food of koalas.

HOARY MARMOT: Marmots are the largest members of the squirrel family. Hoary marmots live in the mountains of northwestern North America. (For more about hoary marmots, see *Danger Joe: Growling Grizzly*.)

HYENA: Hyenas look like dogs, but they are more closely related to cats. They hunt at night in packs and also feed on the kills of other animals. They have short hind legs, very powerful jaws, and coarse hair. Hyenas are very loud animals. They howl and scream and make an eerie noise that sounds like laughter.

KOALA: Koalas are animals from Australia. They have thick gray fur, large ears, sharp claws, and pouches for carrying their young. Koalas spend most of their time in eucalyptus trees, eating leaves. Some people think koalas are bears, but they are not. They are more closely related to kangaroos.

LEOPARD: Leopards are big wildcats. Usually they have tan coats with black spots, but some are all black. Black leopards are sometimes called panthers. Leopards hunt alone and drag their kills into trees to keep them away from hyenas.

ROCK HYRAX: This short, stocky animal is found in Africa and the Middle East. It lives in large groups in rocky areas and eats plants.

SHAMMA: A shamma is a white cotton shawl about five feet wide and ten feet long. It is used to cover the shoulders and arms and sometimes the head. Shammas are often embroidered with brightly colored borders.

SWAHILI: Swahili is the official language of Tanzania, but it is also used as a common language between peoples of different languages in eastern and east-central Africa.

TARANTULA: This name is commonly used for any large hairy spider.

VICTORIA FALLS: Victoria Falls is a waterfall in the Zambezi River in Africa. It falls three hundred and fifty-five feet.

WADI: A wadi is a gully, or riverbed, that is dry except during the rainy season.

WHITE SPOTTED GECKO: The white spotted gecko is an eight-inch-long lizard of northeastern Africa. It feeds on insects, spiders, and other lizards. It uses camouflage to blend in with its surroundings.

ABOUT THE AUTHORS AND ILLUSTRATORS

Creating *The Danger Joe Show* books takes a lot of teamwork. Jon Buller does more of the illustrating, and Susan Schade does more of the writing, but they both do some of each. In addition to their Danger Joe titles, they have published more than forty books, including *20,000 Baseball Cards Under the Sea* and *Space Dog Jack*. They are married and live in Lyme, Connecticut, where they can often be found walking in the local forests, looking for mushrooms, and paddling kayaks in local rivers and streams. They used to have two pet snails, but they decided to release them back into their natural habitat.